CARLYLE
ODERINT DUM METUANT

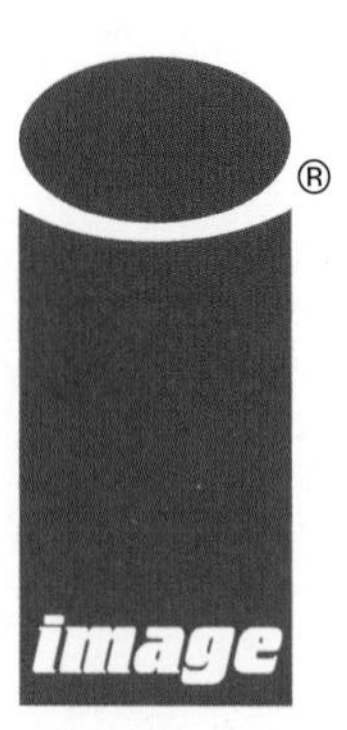

LAZARUS, VOLUME THREE. March 2015. First printing. ISBN: 978-1-63215-225-1. Published by Image Comics, Inc. Office of publication: 2001 Center Street, 6th Floor, Berkeley, CA 94704.

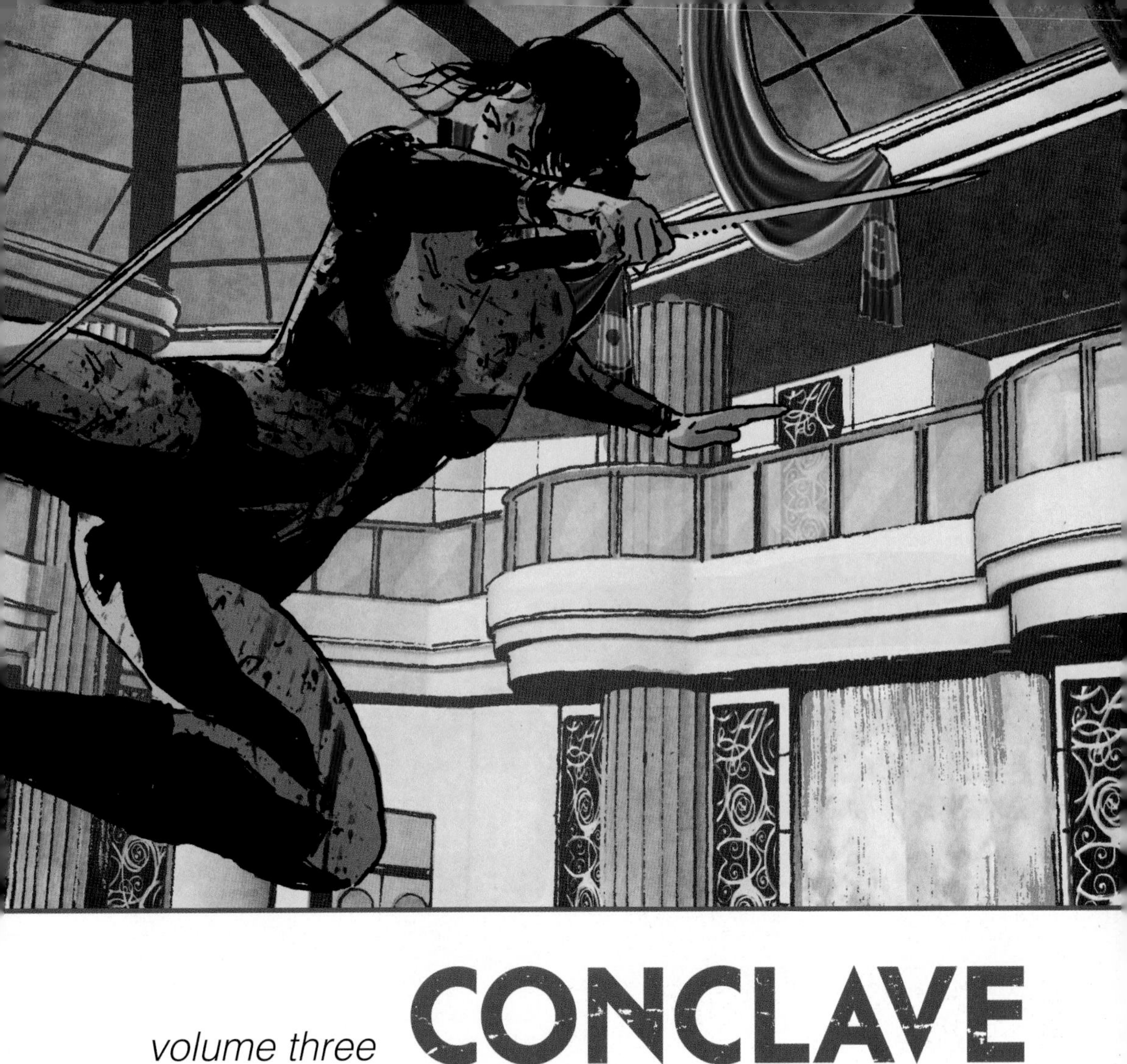

volume three **CONCLAVE**

written by **GREG RUCKA**

art by **MICHAEL LARK**
with **TYLER BOSS**

letters by **JODI WYNNE**

colors by **SANTI ARCAS**

cover by **OWEN FREEMAN**

publication design by **ERIC TRAUTMANN**

edited by **DAVID BROTHERS**

special thanks to **CHRISTOPHER PREECE**

DRAMATIS PERSONAE

FAMILY: Armitage
DOMAIN: United Kingdom of Great Britain and Ireland-made-One
Unallied; close ties to Carlyle.
In conflict with Rausling and D'Souza.

HRH THE DUKE OF LANCASTER EDWARD ARMITAGE
Head of Family Armitage

SIR THOMAS HUSTON
Family Armitage Lazarus

FAMILY: Bittner
DOMAIN: Canada (former provinces of Ontario, Quebec, Newfoundland & Labrador); Northern Europe/North Atlantic (Switzerland, Scandinavia), Germany.
Member of Hock coalition.
In conflict with Carlyle.

SEVARA BITTNER
Head of Family Bittner

SONJA BITTNER
Family Bittner Lazarus

FAMILY: Carlyle
DOMAIN: Western United States (west coast of Alaska contested with Vassalovka); Western Canada; Northern Canada (contested with Bittner).
In conflict with Bittner, Hock, and Vassalovka.
Strong ties with Carragher, Morray, and Nkosi.

MALCOLM CARLYLE
Head of Family Carlyle

CMDR. FOREVER CARLYLE
Family Carlyle Lazarus

DR. BETHANY CARLYLE
Daughter of Malcolm Carlyle

STEPHEN CARLYLE
Son of Malcolm Carlyle

JOHANNA CARLYLE
Daughter of Malcolm Carlyle

JONAH CARLYLE
Son of Malcolm Carlyle, currently held by Jakob Hock

FAMILY: Carragher
DOMAIN: Australia and Indonesia
Member of Carlyle Bloc.
In conflict with Li and Minetta.

LOCHLAN JAMES CARRAGHER VI
Head of Family Carragher

WENING PERTIWI
Family Carragher Lazarus

FAMILY: D'Souza
DOMAIN: Unified South America (Argentina/Brazil/Peru/Chile); Contesting regions of former Venezuela and Colombia with Morray; Spain and Portugal.
Member of Hock Coalition.
In conflict with Morray.

ZEFERINO CARDOSO
Family D'Souza Lazarus

FAMILY: Hock
DOMAIN: United States, east of the Mississippi; portions of the Caribbean; portions of eastern Canada (shared with Bittner).
Allied with Bittner, Vassalovka, Rausling, and D'Souza.
In conflict with Carlyle.

JAKOB HOCK
Head of Family Hock

LI JIAOLONG
Family Li Lazarus.

FAMILY: Li
DOMAIN: China (including Hong Kong and Macau); portions of the Korean Peninsula; Kazakhstan; Mongolia (in dispute with Vassalovka).
Allied with Inamura.
In conflict with Minetta, Vassalovka.

ALIMAH QASIMI
Family Meyers-Qasimi Lazarus.

FAMILY: Meyers-Qasimi
DOMAIN: Former State of Israel/ Palestine through much of the Levant, including former Saudi Arabia,Yemen,and the UAE; Cyprus; Crete.
Unallied, cordial ties with Carlyle.
In conflict with rogue elements operating out of former Soleri (now-ungoverned) territory in North Africa.

BIR CHIKKA MEHTA
Lazarus of Family Minetta

FAMILY: Minetta
DOMAIN: Indian subcontinent, Sri Lanka, former Pakistan; Bangladesh; Myanmar (contested with Li); Thailand and Malaysia (portions, contested with Carragher).
Nominal alliance with Carlyle.
In conflict with Carragher and Li.

EDGAR MORRAY
Head of Family Morray

JOACQUIM MORRAY
Family Morray Lazarus

FAMILY: Morray
DOMAIN: Mexico and Central America, portions of the Caribbean.
Member of Carlyle Bloc.
In conflict with D'Souza and Hock.

XOLANI NKOSI
Family Nkosi Lazarus

FAMILY: Nkosi
DOMAIN: Sub-Saharan Africa below the equator (0°), and Madagascar.
Member of Carlyle Bloc.
In conflict with Martins and rogue elements operating out of former Soleri (now-ungoverned) territory.

LUKA & CLAUDIA RAUSLING
Head of Family Rausling; spouse

CPT. CRISTOF MUELLER
Family Rausling Lazarus

FAMILY: Rausling
DOMAIN: Austria, Poland, portions of Central Europe, between Bittner-controlled Western Europe and Vassalovka-controlled Russia; Greece, excluding Meyers-Qasimi held Crete and Cyprus.
Member of Hock Coalition.
In conflict with Armitage.

MICHAEL LARK

INTERLUDE

EXTRACTION

Four months ago
120 KM West of the Mississippi
Family: Carlyle
BITCH.

YOU BITCH.
YOU BITCH YOU BITCH YOU BITCH--
--YOUBITCHBITCHBITCH JOHANNA--

I TRUSTED YOU.
YOU'RE MY SISTER.

I LOVE YOU.

Warning:

Fuel reserves at ten percent.

Mississippi River, East Bank
Family: Hock
Population: 27 (Hock Militia Unit)
HEY?
THAT.
WHAT?
HUH.
HALF-DOZEN WASPS SAYS HE DOESN'T MAKE THE WATER.
NO BET, MAN.
YEAH.
I WOULDN'T TAKE THAT BET, EITHER.

--at zero percent.
I KNOW!
Warning: Stall.
I FUCKING KNOW!
Warning: Impact imminent.
I KNO--

uhnn
uff

UHM, HEY?

YOU GUYS GOT A **BOAT?**
SO I CAN GET ACROSS?
AH, NO, SIR.
NO BOATS.

GONNA HAVE TO SWIM.
NO BOATS.
SERIOUSLY?
YOU DON'T WANT TO SWALLOW ANY OF THAT.
IT'S ALL SHIT AND PISS.
FUCKING LOVELY, JUST--
--GAH!

OH JESUS CHRIST, THAT'S DISGUSTING!
THAT'S JUST FOUL, THAT'S--
--THANK YOU, THANKS...
...OH THANK GOD, WARMTH.
I'LL JUST STAND HERE FOR A MOMENT, IF YOU DON'T MIND?
DO YOU HAVE A PHONE?
A PHONE?
OR A RADIO? I NEED TO SPEAK TO SOMEONE IN YOUR COMMAND.
MY NAME'S JONAH CARLYLE, I NEED TO SPEAK TO JAKOB HOCK.
HE'LL WANT TO KNOW I'M HERE. I'M SEEKING ASYLUM.
I'M VERY IMPORTANT, HE'LL LIKELY REWARD YOU ALL FOR...
...YOUR SERVICE--

...NOSIR, I UNDERSTAND...
...NOT A HAIR ON HIS HEAD, YESSIR.
THEY'RE SENDING SOMEONE FROM THE MINISTRY OF SAFETY TO PICK HIM UP.
WE'RE SUPPOSED TO TAKE CARE OF HIM.
HOW'RE WE SUPPOSED TO DO THAT, MAN?
MAKE HIM DINNER?
FUCK IF I KNOW.
GIVE HIM HIS CLOTHES BACK, I SUPPOSE.
TELL YOU ONE THING, THOUGH...
...I'M KEEPING THE SHOES.

GET YOUR HANDS OFF ME!
DON'T YOU KNOW WHO I AM?
HOCK
I DEMAND TO SPEAK TO JAKOB HOCK!
ARE YOU LISTENING TO ME?
HE WANTS TO TALK TO ME! I'M OFFERING TO HELP HIM!
DAMMIT! ANSWER ME! I DEMAND--

Manhattan
Family: Hock
Population [Family]: 1
Population [Citizens]: 750,000 (approx)
Population [Non-Persons]: 1,375,500 (approx)
SAFETY
TRUST IN HOCK
TAKE YOUR MEDICINE
YOUR LABOR
YOU ARE UNDER SURVEILLANCE
OH GOD THANK GOD...
...JUST...LISTEN TO ME. LISTEN!
I'M NOT--I'M NOT SOME WASTE, YOU UNDERSTAND? I'M AN IMPORTANT--
--WH-WHAT ARE YOU DOING?

STOP! YOU CAN'T DO THIS!
I WANT TO TALK TO JAKOB HOCK! I'M JONAH CARLYLE, I WANT TO--
D HOCK TERRITORY
...stop...
...my name...my name is Jonah Carlyle...
...don't...
...don't do this...
PLEASE.
I'M JONAH CARLYLE....

SUBJECT DESIGNATE:
LOGGED
...MY NAME IS JONAH CARLYLE...
...I WANT TO SPEAK TO JAKOB HOCK...
...I'M SEEKING ASYLUM...
...FROM MY FAMILY...
...PLEASE, SOMEBODY...
...SOMEBODY ANSWER ME--

YOU HAVE ENTERED ROCK TERRITORY
INTAKE
DECON

AVOID CONTAMINATION
WASH THOROUGHLY

HEALTH IS HAPPINESS
TAKE YOUR MEDICINE

...DECISIVE GAINS BY VALIANT HOCK FAMILY FORCES IN THEIR WAR AGAINST MALCOLM CARLYLE.
HERE, MEMBERS OF THE 17th HOCK ELITES CAN BE SEEN ROUTING THE ENEMY OUTSIDE OF DENVER...
...LEADING TO THE DISCOVERY OF ANOTHER OF CARLYLE'S **SLAVE LABOR** CAMPS, WHERE TENS OF THOUSANDS HAVE BEEN FORCED TO TOIL UNTO DEATH.
ALWAYS OBEY
WOMEN AND CHILDREN RESCUED FROM THE SITE DETAIL HORRIFIC FORCED-BREEDING PROGRAMS...
...AND GROTESQUE **SEXUAL ABUSES** PERPETRATED BY MEMBERS OF THE CARLYLE FAMILY.
THAT'S... THAT'S NOT TRUE.
THIS JUST IN:
THE FAMILY MORRAY DECLARES ALLEGIANCE TO HOCK AGAINST THE CARLYLE MENACE!
IN CELEBRATION, ALL CITIZENS WILL RECEIVE AN AUGMENTATION TO THEIR **HEALTH ALLOTMENT...**
TAKE YOUR MEDICINE
...WITH AN INCREASE OF TWO BLUES, THREE WHITES, AND SIX BLACK-AND-YELLOWS.
REMEMBER, CITIZENS: TAKE YOUR **MEDICINE.**
ALWAYS OBEY

LOOK AT YOU...

...HAS TO BE AT LEAST FORTY YEARS SINCE I SAW YOU LAST, AND YOU DON'T LOOK A DAY OLDER.
COME AND SIT, JONAH.

YOU MUST BE STARVING.
YEAH, I AM.
I CAN'T SAY MUCH FOR YOUR HOSPITALITY, DOCTOR HOCK.
THE WAY I'VE BEEN TREATED AND EVERYTHING.
I'LL SEE IF I CAN'T MAKE IT UP TO YOU.
I'M TIRED, I'M HUNGRY, I'M HURTING, I DON'T WANT TO PLAY GAMES WITH YOU, JAKOB.
THERE ARE THINGS I WANT. I'M PREPARED TO GIVE YOU A LOT OF INFORMATION FOR THEM.
SO YOU'VE BEEN HEARD TO SAY.
BUT WHAT I WANT YOU CANNOT POSSIBLY TELL ME.
YOU CAN'T KNOW THAT UNTIL YOU HEAR ME OUT.
ON THIS I BELIEVE I CAN, JONAH.
I MEAN, WHAT IS IT YOU DO FOR YOUR FAMILY? ASIDE FROM TRYING TO PUT IT IN YOUR SISTER, I MEAN?
I DIDN'T--

YOU DON'T DO ANYTHING, DO YOU?
GIVE HIM THIS.
I RAN THE LOS ANGELES DOMAIN FOR MY FAMILY!
NOT SOMETHING I WOULD PUT ON MY RESUMÉ.
SWALLOW THAT, PLEASE.
RIGHT, BECAUSE I'M AN IDIOT.
NO WAY.
YOU ARE AN IDIOT, JONAH.
YOU HAVE WORTH, JUST NOT THE WORTH YOU THINK.
WHAT YOU KNOW IS MEANINGLESS TO ME, BECAUSE YOU KNOW NOTHING.
WHAT YOU ARE IS USEFUL, HOWEVER.
NOW: TAKE YOUR MEDICINE.

FUCK YOU.
YOU'RE LEAVING?
WHERE ARE YOU GOING TO GO, JONAH?
TING-TING
HOLD HIM.
DON'T TOUCH ME.
DON'T!
THERE ARE SECRETS LOCKED WITHIN YOUR BODY, JONAH.
SECRETS YOUR FATHER HAS KEPT FROM ME FOR OVER SIXTY YEARS...
...SECRETS YOU WILL HELP ME UNCOVER.

DOCTOR HOCK--
--JAKOB, C'MON, I CAME TO YOU FOR HELP!
OH, YOU CAME SEEKING CHARITY?
NO, YOU CAME TO BARGAIN...
...AND YOU HAD NOTHING WITH WHICH TO DEAL.
TAKE YOUR MEDICINE, JONAH...
...IT'LL MAKE THINGS SO MUCH EASIER FOR YOU IF YOU DO.

GOOD.
WHAT...
...WHAT ARE YOU GOING TO DO?
I'M GOING TO BE YOUNG AGAIN.
AND YOU'RE GOING TO HELP. YOU WANT TO HELP, DON'T YOU, JONAH?
YES.
I KNEW YOU WOULD.
TAKE HIM DOWN TO MY LAB AND PREP HIM.

I'LL NEED ONE OF HIS FINGERS.
RIGHT RING FINGER WILL DO.
MAKE SURE YOU PUT IT ON ICE.
SECURE, MEDICINE MAN PROTOCOL, ENCRYPTION NINE.
CALL THE BITCH.
BONJOUR, DOCTEUR HOCK. COMMENT ÇA-VA?
LIVE SESSION
ÇA-VA BIEN, MERCI, NATASCHA.
PUIS-JE PARLER AVEC VOTRE MÈRE, S'IL VOUS PLAÎT?
JUSTE UN INSTANT.

JAKOB.
WHAT CAN I DO FOR YOU?
NOT FOR **ME,** SEVARA. FOR **US.**
AN **OPPORTUNITY** HAS PRESENTED ITSELF TO FORWARD **BOTH** OUR HOUSES, MY DEAR.
MALCOLM HAS **FINALLY** MADE A MISCALCULATION.
ONE THAT WE CAN **EXPLOIT.**
MALCOLM CARLYLE DOES NOT **MAKE** MISCALCULATIONS, JAKOB.
PERHAPS **NOT,** BUT HIS **CHILDREN** ARE ANOTHER MATTER.
AND WHAT DO YOU THINK HE MIGHT BE WILLING TO DO TO GET ONE OF THEM **BACK?**
I SHOULD THINK ALMOST **ANYTHING.**
AND THE ACCORDS ARE VERY **CLEAR** ON THE MATTER OF **RANSOM.**
YES, THEY ARE. YES, THEY ARE...

"...I THINK THE TIME HAS COME FOR A CONCLAVE, SEVARA DEAR...
"...AND ONCE ALL THE FAMILIES HAVE GATHERED TOGETHER...
"...WE SHALL HAVE THE MEANS TO DESTROY CARLYLE ONCE AND FOR ALL..."

CARLYLE
ODERINT DUM METUANT

OWEN FREEMAN

CONCLAVE
CHAPTER ONE

Southwest Ontario, approximately 80 KM NNE of Lake of the Woods
Monitored Carlyle/Bittner Border
FOXTROT BIRD'S EYE, VICTOR-12, INCURSION VERIFIED...
Family: Carlyle
...LOCATE AND INTERCEPT.
FOXTROT, WE HAVE EYES ON...
Population [Serf]: 108
...WILL UPDATE, STAND-BY.
350
300
250
200
150
DISTANCE: 51.2 M
DIRECTION: SW
SE S SW W NW
HOLY SHIT...
Population [Waste]: Data Unavailable.
...YOU KNOW WHO I THINK THAT IS?

I THINK THAT'S A FUCKING LAZARUS.
I THINK THAT'S SONJA FUCKING BITTNER, MAN.
350
300
250
200
150
DISTANCE 8.8 M
DIRECTION: NW
SE S W NW
SHIT! SHIT SHIT SHIT...
...HALT! JUST--JUST STOP!
THIS IS CARLYLE TERRITORY, UNAUTHORIZED ENTRY WITHOUT A TRAVEL PERMIT IS FORBIDDEN.
HALT! HALT OR I WILL SHOOT!
I AM SONJA BITTNER, AND I AM SENT BY MY MOTHER.
I AM TO DELIVER A GIFT TO THE FAMILY CARLYLE.
LAY YOUR SWORD AND RIFLE ON THE ROAD.
I AM SENT BY MY MOTHER WITH A GIFT FOR CARLYLE.
STOP! SURRENDER YOUR WEAPONS!
SHE CAN'T, MAN! YOU'RE ASKING HER TO--

gnh
MY NAME IS SONJA BITTNER.
I AM SENT BY MY MOTHER WITH A GIFT FOR CARLYLE.
TELL THEM I AM HERE.

Southern Sierra Nevadas
Facility: Compound Sequoia
Family: Carlyle
"OKAY, FOREVER, HERE'S WHAT WE'VE GOT...
Population [Family]: 3 [1 permanent]
"...YOUR SISTER AND I HAVE FINISHED CRUNCHING THE NUMBERS ON YOUR PERFORMANCE REVIEW...
Population [Serf]: 32
"...AND I HAVE TO TELL YOU, WE'RE VERY PLEASED WITH THE RESULTS.
"YOU'RE CONTINUING TO PERFORM ABOVE ALL OF OUR PROJECTIONS, AND IN FACT THE GROWTH CURVE ON YOUR ABILITIES SEEMS TO BE ACCELERATING...

...SO MUCH SO THAT BETHANY AND I ARE THINKING IT'S TIME TO ACTIVATE ONE OR TWO OF THE DORMANT GENETIC PACKAGES YOU'VE BEEN CARRYING.
IF THEY WORK, AND WE'VE NO REASON TO THINK THEY WON'T--
THEY'LL WORK, JAMES.
YOUR CONFIDENCE IS OVERWHELMING AS ALWAYS, BETH.
WHAT WAS I SAYING?
THE NEW PACKAGES.
RIGHT, YES, THEY'LL BOOST YOUR ENVIRONMENTAL RESISTANCES. COLD, HEAT, RADIATION, TOXINS.
A FEW OTHER SURPRISES, TOO.
YOU'RE NOT EVEN LISTENING TO ME, ARE YOU?
CAN I ASK YOU, SOMETHING, JAMES?
ALWAYS, EVE.
AM I A CARLYLE?

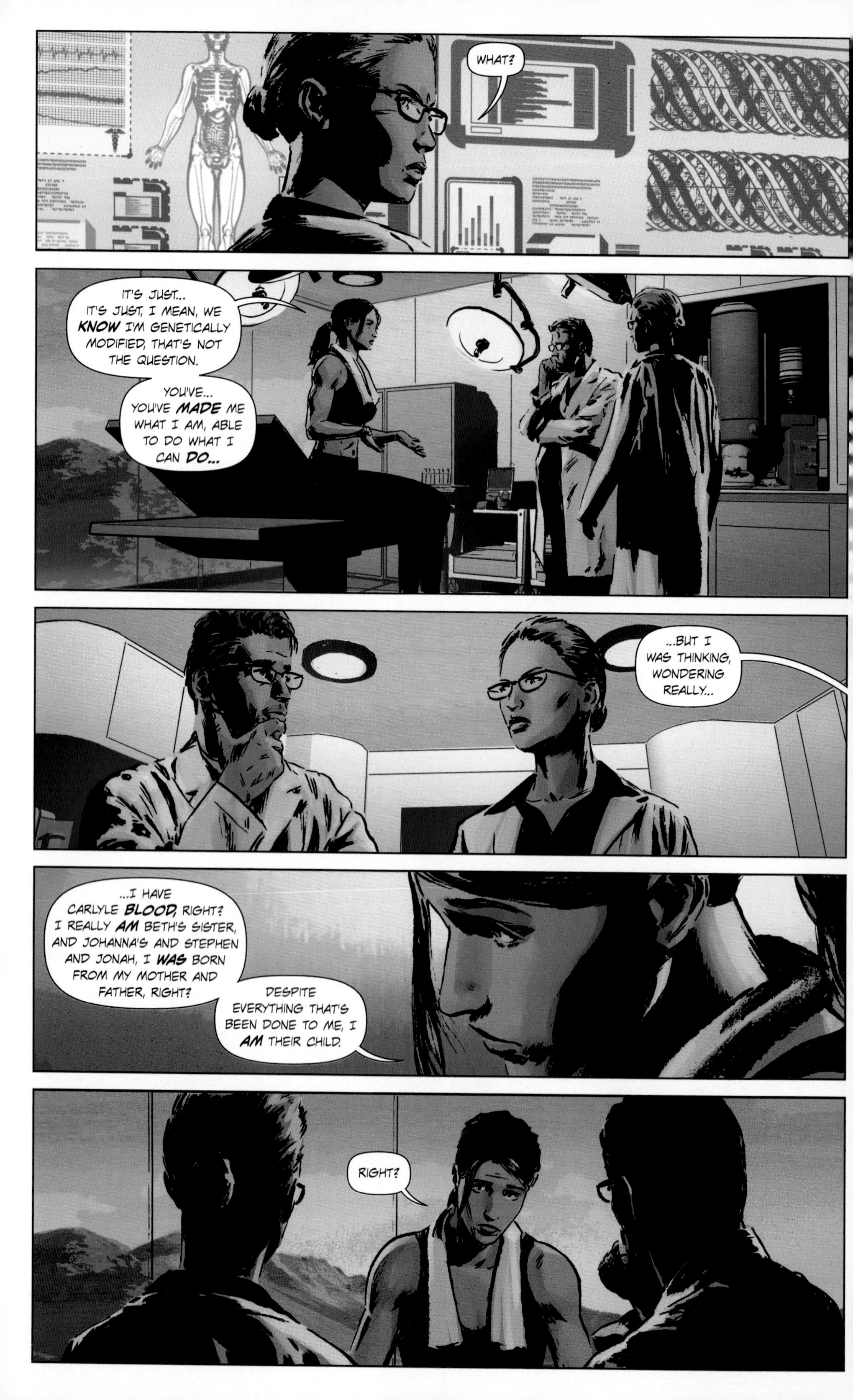
WHAT?
IT'S JUST... IT'S JUST, I MEAN, WE KNOW I'M GENETICALLY MODIFIED, THAT'S NOT THE QUESTION.
YOU'VE... YOU'VE MADE ME WHAT I AM, ABLE TO DO WHAT I CAN DO...
...BUT I WAS THINKING, WONDERING REALLY...
...I HAVE CARLYLE BLOOD, RIGHT? I REALLY AM BETH'S SISTER, AND JOHANNA'S AND STEPHEN AND JONAH, I WAS BORN FROM MY MOTHER AND FATHER, RIGHT?
DESPITE EVERYTHING THAT'S BEEN DONE TO ME, I AM THEIR CHILD.
RIGHT?

OH MY GOD!
ARE YOU ASKING IF YOU'RE ADOPTED?
SWEETIE, I WAS THERE WHEN YOU WERE BORN!
YOU'RE ONE-HUNDRED PERCENT CARLYLE, BELIEVE ME!
YEAH. I KNOW, IT'S... IT'S SILLY, I GUESS...
IT KINDA IS, I HAVE TO SAY. WHERE'S THIS COMING FROM, YOU ASKING QUESTIONS LIKE THAT OUT OF THE BLUE?
I JUST... I WAS JUST WONDERING, THAT'S ALL, BETH.
THAT'S ALL.
I'M GOING TO GO GET CLEANED UP...

ZONE KAPPA
AUTHORIZED PERSONNEL ONLY
ZONE KAPPA

SHE NEVER CALLS, SHE NEVER WRITES...

NEVER.
...IT'S ENOUGH TO MAKE A GIRL THINK SHE'S BEEN FORGOTTEN.

NEVER NOT EVER, MARISOL.
NOT EVER.
GOD, LOOK AT YOU. YOU JUST KEEP GROWING.
WHAT HAS IT BEEN, TWO YEARS?
ABOUT THAT, YES.
I DIDN'T KNOW YOU WERE HERE. I THOUGHT YOU WERE AT PENDLETON.
AND LAST I HEARD, YOU WERE BABYSITTING JO IN LOS ANGELES.
NAH, I'M BACK HERE FOR TREATMENT...
...ANOTHER BOOSTER TO KEEP MY TITS HIGH AND MY ASS TIGHT.
NONE HIGHER NOR TIGHTER.
FOR A WOMAN COMING UP ON NINETY YOU HAVE TO ADMIT, I LOOK DAMN GOOD.
YES, YOU DO.
ZONE KAPPA
YOU'RE NOT EVEN SUPPOSED TO BE IN THIS WING.
TAKING A WALK DOWN MEMORY LANE?
I GUESS SO.
HAD A LOT ON MY MIND.
I'M HAPPY TO TALK, HAPPY TO LISTEN....
KAPPA
ONE GAMMA

HAVE YOU BACK-TRACED IT?
TO: CARLYLE_FOREVER
HE IS NOT YOUR FATHER.
THIS IS NOT YOUR FAMILY.
I TRIED DOING IT MYSELF, BUT NONE OF THE SOFTWARE COULD CRACK IT.
YOU COULD KICK IT OVER TO THE BASILISK TEAM. I'M SURE THEY COULD FIGURE OUT WHO SENT IT.
I THOUGHT ABOUT IT.
BUT YOU DIDN'T. WHY NOT?
BECAUSE I DON'T WANT ANYONE TO THINK I'M TAKING IT SERIOUSLY.
ARE YOU?
I SEE.

YOU NEED TO BRING THIS TO YOUR FATHER, FOREVER.
AT BEST, THIS MEANS SOMEONE'S COMPROMISED YOUR COMS. AT WORST, WHOEVER SENT IT IS TRYING TO PLAY PSYOPS ON YOU.
OH, I KNOW WHO SENT IT.
JONAH SENT IT.
WHEREVER HE IS NOW, WHOEVER HE'S BETRAYED US TO...
...IT'S HIS LITTLE FUCK YOU TO ME, I'M SURE OF IT.
COULD YOU GET THAT, PLEASE?
SURE.
INCOMING CALL
COMMANDER? MY NAME IS CAPTAIN LUCE, CHARLIE COMPANY, THIRD BATTALION, BORDER WATCH...
...I, UH... I'M SORRY TO BOTHER YOU, BUT WE'VE GOT A SITUATION HERE...
...AND PROTOCOL SAYS I'M TO CONTACT YOU DIRECTLY IN CASES LIKE THIS, SO...
WHAT CAN I DO FOR YOU, CAPTAIN?
WELL, THAT'S THE THING.
THERE'S... THERE'S SOMEONE OUT HERE WHO WANTS TO SPEAK WITH YOU....

SHE SAYS SHE HAS A GIFT FOR YOUR FAMILY.
I JUST, I DIDN'T KNOW WHAT ELSE TO DO, I DIDN'T WANT TO START AN INCIDENT WITH BITTNER OR--
THANK YOU, CAPTAIN LUCE.
CARLYLE WILL STAND DOWN.
I SPEAK FOR CARLYLE.
I SPEAK FOR BITTNER.
YOUR PURPOSE IS SERVED.

I AM BITTNER. I AM THE VOICE OF MY FAMILY.
MY MOTHER SPEAKS:
"WE COME TO YOU, OUR ADVERSARY, ON BEHALF OF ANOTHER," MY MOTHER SAYS.
"WE COME TO CARLYLE ACTING AT THE BEHEST OF HOCK, THAT FAMILY YOU HAVE SO CRUELLY WRONGED."
"IN HOCK'S POSSESSION IS THAT WHICH YOU HAVE LOST."
"IN HOCK'S POSSESSION IS THAT WHICH YOU SEEK TO RECOVER."
MY MOTHER SPEAKS, "HOCK WOULD RETURN THAT WHICH HAS BEEN MISLAID...
"...THAT CHILD OF CARLYLE NAMED JONAH...

"...FOR A PRICE."
THIS MY MOTHER SPEAKS, ON BEHALF OF HOCK.
I AM TO AWAIT YOUR REPLY.
COMMANDER?
GIVE HER ALL COMFORT AND COURTESIES.

Puget Sound – The Center
Population [Family]: 3 (2 Permanent)
...CAN'T DETERMINE IF IT'S HIS FINGER OR NOT, FATHER...
...AT LEAST NOT UNTIL I CAN GET IT BACK TO SEQUOIA.
OH, I'M SURE IT IS.
INTERESTING THAT JAKOB WENT TO BITTNER, AND NOT VASSALOVKA.
YOU KNEW.
YOU KNEW THIS WOULD HAPPEN.
IN TRUTH, I EXPECTED THE RANSOM DEMAND TWO MONTHS AGO.
THAT'S WHY YOU LET JONAH GO.
THAT'S WHY YOU DIDN'T SEND ME AFTER HIM.

IF WE FOLLOW THE ACCORDS, WE HAVE TWO OPTIONS.
DO YOU RECALL WHAT THEY ARE, DAUGHTER?
WE CAN PAY THE RANSOM.
OR WE CAN BRING IT TO THE OTHER FAMILIES.
AND OF COURSE, THE **THIRD** OPTION.
OPEN CONFLICT, YES.
AND JAKOB HOCK KNOWS THIS AS WELL AS WE DO. SO WHAT WOULD YOU ADVISE ME?
...I...
I WOULD...
I WOULD... ADVISE AGAINST **ANY** NEGOTIATION WITH HOCK WITHOUT ANOTHER FAMILY ACTING AS **ARBITER.**
...YOU WANT TO CALL A **CONCLAVE.**
YOU WANT **ALL** THE FAMILIES BROUGHT TOGETHER FOR THIS.
THAT IS PRECISELY WHAT I WANT, YES.
TELL THE BITTNER LAZARUS THIS, EXACTLY...

"...THAT I DEMAND A **CONCLAVE,** AS ALLOWED BY THE ACCORDS OF MACAU IN ARTICLE FOUR, SUBSECTION THREE.
"SHE WILL EXPECT THIS, FOREVER. SHE WILL AGREE, THEN PROPOSE THE HOST BE EITHER VASSALOVKA OR D'SOUZA.
"TELL HER NEITHER IS ACCEPTABLE, THAT VASSALOVKA IS IN CONFLICT WITH OUR ALLY CARRAGHER, AND D'SOUZA WITH OUR ALLY MORRAY.
"SHE WILL EXPECT YOU TO OFFER AN ALTERNATIVE. DON'T. LET HER SPEAK NEXT.
"HOCK WON'T WANT THE CONCLAVE HOSTED BY ANY OF THE ASIANS, NOR MINETTA, AND BITTNER WON'T WANT TO GO TO AFRICA.
"THE PAUSE WILL BE AWKWARD. BE PATIENT.
"EVENTUALLY, SHE WILL PROPOSE EITHER MEYERS OR ARMITAGE. LET HER THINK YOU ARE CONSIDERING THE CHOICE BEFORE RELUCTANTLY AGREEING TO ARMITAGE.
"SET THE DATE OF THE CONCLAVE FOR A WEEK FROM TODAY.
"INSIST ON SMALL DELEGATIONS, NO MORE THAN FIVE MEMBERS FROM EACH FAMILY INCLUDING PERSONAL SECURITY AND ADVISORS.
"THAT SHOULD CONCLUDE YOUR DIALOGUE.
"GRANT HER SAFE PASSAGE AND THEN RETURN TO THE CENTER...

"...WE HAVE MUCH TO DO AND NOT MUCH TIME IN WHICH TO DO IT."
--YOU GO? HE'S MY TWIN BROTHER!
BECAUSE FOREVER IS GOING, YOU PRISSY LITTLE IDIOT! SHE'S GOT TO BE MAINTAINED!
LISTEN TO YOURSELF! SHE'S OUR SISTER--
--SHE'S NOT A FUCKING CAR, BETH!
BETHANY WILL COME, JOHANNA WILL STAY.
THE REST OF OUR DELEGATION WILL CONSIST OF DOCTOR MANN, ARTHUR COHN, AND FOREVER.
DADDY! PLEASE!
YOUR DOMAIN REQUIRES YOUR ATTENTION, JOHANNA.
STEPHEN, YOU'RE IN CHARGE OF DAY-TO-DAY OPERATIONS WHILST WE'RE AWAY.
I EXPECT YOU TO LOOK AFTER YOUR MOTHER.
YOU MAY RELY ON ME, FATHER.

SHOULDN'T YOU BE GETTING READY?
I NEED TO TALK TO YOU ABOUT FOREVER.
IS SHE ALL RIGHT?
SHE'S FINE, SHE'S BETTER THAN FINE, SHE'S OPERATING ABOVE ALL OUR PROJECTIONS AND MODELS FOR THIS STAGE OF GROWTH.
BUT SHE'S STARTING TO ASK QUESTIONS, FATHER. SHE ASKED JAMES AND ME IF SHE'S REALLY A CARLYLE...
...IF SHE'S REALLY YOUR DAUGHTER.
DID SHE?
DID SHE SAY WHY?
NO, SHE WAS EVASIVE. SAID SHE'D BEEN THINKING ABOUT THE GENETICS, THE WORK DONE TO HER.
I SEE.
SOMEONE PUT THAT QUESTION IN HER HEAD, BETH. SOMEONE IS MAKING TROUBLE...

"...FIND OUT WHO..."
HEY, HEY! SLOW DOWN!
IT'S A CONCLAVE, NOT A WAR, RIGHT?
ONE CAN LEAD TO THE OTHER.
ONLY IF THAT'S WHAT DAD'S AFTER.
LISTEN, I DON'T KNOW WHAT DAD IS PLAYING AT, WHAT HE HOPES TO GAIN FROM THIS.
BUT JONAH USED US, FOREVER. HE LIED TO US.
HE BEAT ME.
REMEMBER THAT...

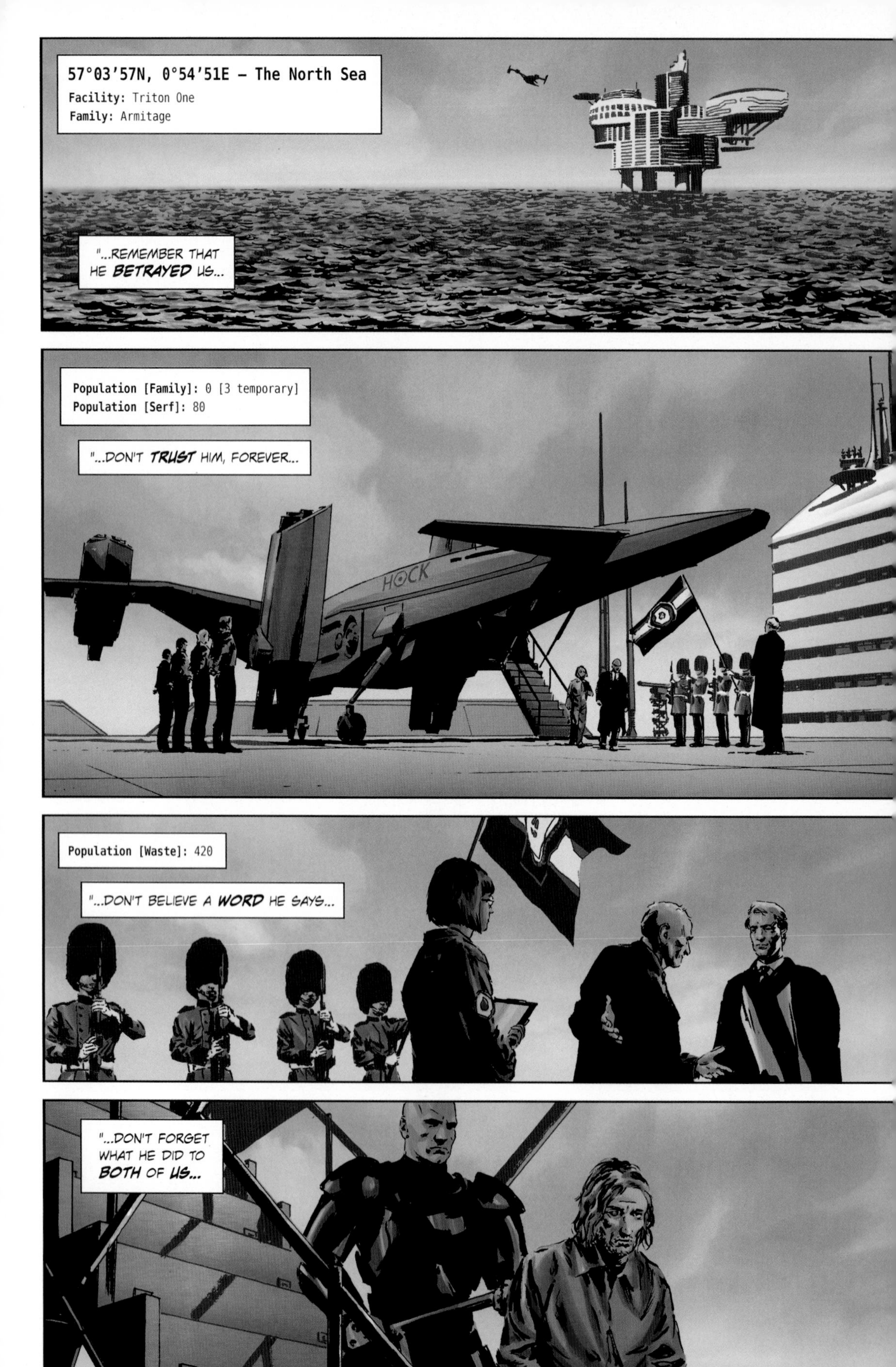
57°03'57N, 0°54'51E – The North Sea
Facility: Triton One
Family: Armitage
"...REMEMBER THAT HE BETRAYED US...
Population [Family]: 0 [3 temporary]
Population [Serf]: 80
"...DON'T TRUST HIM, FOREVER...
HOCK
Population [Waste]: 420
"...DON'T BELIEVE A WORD HE SAYS...
"...DON'T FORGET WHAT HE DID TO BOTH OF US...
"...HE'S NOT OUR BROTHER ANYMORE..."

CARLYLE
ODERINT DUM METUANT

MICHAEL LARK & OWEN FREEMAN

CONCLAVE
CHAPTER TWO

57°03'57N, 0°54'51E – The North Sea
Facility: Triton One
...HOCK'S COALITION WE COULD FIND OURSELVES WITHOUT SUPPORT, MALCOLM.
Family: Armitage
Population [Family]: 0 [3 temporary]
Population [Serf]: 80
Population [Waste]: 420
WE DO HAVE OUR OWN ALLIES, ARTHUR.
THANK YOU.
FOR THE MOMENT. RIGHT NOW, HOCK HAS AT LEAST FOUR FAMILIES AT HIS BACK...
...BITTNER, VASSALOVKA, D'SOUZA, AND MARTINS.
FIVE.
YOU'RE FORGETTING RAUSLING, ARTHUR.
I HAVEN'T BEEN ABLE TO CONFIRM THAT AS YET.
OH, I THINK IT'S COMMON SENSE...

...RAUSLING'S EXPOSED ON ALL FRONTS OTHERWISE.
THANK YOU, FOREVER.
BY THE SAME LOGIC, WE'LL LOSE MORRAY.
I'D BE STUNNED IF HOCK HASN'T ALREADY MADE OVERTURES.
PROMISING TO KEEP D'SOUZA OFF HIS SOUTHERN BORDER?
THAT, OR GRANTING HIM OUR TERRITORY ONCE WE'RE EXTINCT.
THANK YOU, FOREVER.
YOU'RE VERY WELCOME, MISTER COHN.
FOREVER...
...WHAT DO YOU THINK?
FATHER?

YOU'VE LISTENED TO ARTHUR AND I DISCUSS THIS ALL MORNING.
SURELY YOU'VE FORMED SOME OPINIONS OF YOUR OWN?
CARRAGHER AND NKOSI CAN BE COUNTED ON TO STAND WITH US NO MATTER WHAT.
BUT MUCH AS I HATE TO ADMIT IT, I THINK MISTER COHN'S ASSESSMENT ON MORRAY IS CORRECT.
HOCK HAS HAD JONAH PRISONER AT LEAST FOUR MONTHS.
IS THAT LONG ENOUGH TO HAVE CRACKED THE LONGEVITY CODE?
THAT'S THE BILLION DOLLAR QUESTION.
IF HOCK CAN PROMISE THE OTHER FAMILIES EFFECTIVE IMMORTALITY, EVERY SINGLE ONE OF THEM WILL RALLY TO HIS SIDE.
CLASSIFIED
YOU'RE BOTH FORGETTING THE GRAIN.
AND IF THEIR WASTE STARVE, THOSE FAMILIES ARE ALL IMMEDIATELY FIGHTING ON TWO FRONTS.
I'M NOT FORGETTING THAT, MALCOLM.
I'M JUST NOT CERTAIN THAT WOULD STOP THEM.

HOCK WILL HAVE TO CONVINCE THE OTHER FAMILIES HE NOW HAS WHAT THEY WANT.
IT HAS TO BE PUBLIC. HE'LL DO IT TONIGHT, HE'LL DO IT AT THE OPENING GALA.
ASK EDGAR MORRAY AND JAMES CARRAGHER TO JOIN ME FOR LUNCH, PLEASE, ARTHUR.
AND LET ME KNOW WHEN SEVARA BITTNER CALLS.
SEVARA BITTNER IS ALLIED WITH HOCK.

AT PRESENT, YES.

I WANT YOU TO TAKE SOME TIME BEFORE THE GALA TONIGHT, TRY TO RELAX.
I THOUGHT I WOULD CHECK SECURITY--
YOU'RE NOT HEARING ME, DAUGHTER...

...ARMITAGE'S PEOPLE HAVE THAT WELL IN HAND. TAKE SOME TIME FOR YOURSELF...

"...TRY TO RELAX, TRY TO ENJOY YOURSELF..."

VERY NICE, SONJA.

YOU ARE KIND, FOREVER.
THANK YOU.

YOU MADE IT **HOME** OKAY? NO TROUBLE WITH OUR PEOPLE?
NO TROUBLES AT ALL. I WAS GIVEN EVERY COURTESY.

WOULD YOU LIKE TO JOIN ME?

I'D LOVE TO, SONJA.

MY YOUNGER SISTER IS AT THE SPA. SHE SAID IT WOULD BE WASTED ON ME.
I THOUGHT I WOULD BE ALONE DOWN HERE.
MY FATHER TOLD ME I SHOULD ENJOY MYSELF AND TRY TO RELAX.
IT WAS KIND OF MISTER ARMITAGE TO GIVE US A PLACE TO PRACTICE.
DUKE EDWARD DIDN'T DO IT OUT OF KINDNESS, SONJA.
HE DOESN'T WANT US IN THE HEALTH SPA WITH THE REST OF THE FAMILIES.
SECURITY, YOU MEAN?
THAT'S THE EXCUSE.
THEN WHAT IS THE TRUE REASON?
THEY'RE SCARED SHITLESS OF US.

ISN'T THAT RIGHT, FOREVER?

XOLANI. YOU GOT **TALL.**
YEAH, WELL YOU GOT TALL **AND** TITS.
WEARING **BOTH** VERY NICELY, FAR AS THAT GOES.

SONJA, YOU KNOW XOLANI NKOSI?

NO, I DO NOT. MY FAMILY AND NKOSI ARE--
--ADVERSARIES? IT'S NOT THE **RACE** THING, IS IT?
MY FATHER SAYS IT'S THE **RACE** THING.

NO! NO, MISTER NKOSI, IT IS...
...WE ARE **ALLIES** WITH MARTINS IN AFRICA, AS YOU KNOW, THAT IS **WHY** AND--
XOLANI. I'M JUST TAKING THE PISS, THAT'S ALL.
SO...

...ANYONE FOR **TENNIS?**

--THE NEW ONE, SHOULD BE THERE TONIGHT.
RAWLING, YES, I'D HEARD.
SWITCH.

SIR THOMAS IS PUTTING ON ONE OF HIS POKER GAMES FOR LATE. I THINK HE'S HOPING TO TAKE HIS MEASURE.
TAKE HIM TO THE CLEANERS, YOU MEAN.
SWITCH.

I WISH I COULD GO.
AGAINST YOUR MOTHER'S WISHES?
I DON'T KNOW HOW TO PLAY.

I'D BE HAPPY TO TEACH YOU.

I--I SHOULD-- I MEAN, WE SHOULD PROBABLY BE GETTING READY FOR THE GALA.

WE PROBABLY SHOULD.

DINNER.
DOCTOR HOCK WANTS YOU TO EAT.
WHAT'D HE PUT IN IT THIS TIME?
DOESN'T MATTER.
YOU'LL EAT IT ANYWAY.

YOU'RE STAYING HERE TONIGHT.

I DOUBT HE HAS THE WHEREWITHAL, BUT SHOULD YOUNG MASTER CARLYLE GET ANY IDEAS, I EXPECT YOU TO PUT A STOP TO THEM.

YES, SIR.

GOOD BOY. TIME FOR YOUR MEDICINE.

CHKSS

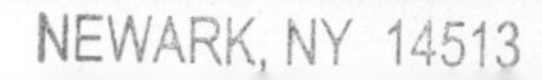

BETH?
FATHER?
JAMES KNOWS TO WEAR HIS TUX?
ARTHUR'S HELPING HIM WITH THE TIE RIGHT NOW.
SIXTY YEARS AND HE STILL CAN'T TIE A BOW TIE.
YOU LOOK VERY NICE, BY THE WAY.
THANK YOU, FATHER.
WILL HOCK PRESENT JONAH TONIGHT? SHOW HIM TO US?
NO, IT WOULD BE A DISTRACTION.
WE'VE CONFIRMED JONAH IS HERE, THAT'S ENOUGH.
WHERE'S YOUR SISTER?
HERE, I'M HERE...

...I CAN'T...
...I'M HAVING TROUBLE WITH THIS DAMN DRESS.
MAY I JUST WEAR MY UNIFORM INSTEAD, FATHER?
PLEASE?
THIS IS A BLACK-TIE GALA, FOREVER...
...THE DRESS IS APPROPRIATE.
I'M GOING TO LOOK STUPID. I WON'T BE ABLE TO WEAR MY SWORD.
YOU'RE GOING TO LOOK BRILLIANT, AND THE ONLY WEAPONS TONIGHT ARE CEREMONIAL, SO YOU DON'T NEED IT.
BETH, WOULD YOU PLEASE HELP YOUR SISTER?
COME ON, SILLY. SERIOUSLY...
...YOU CAN SURVIVE KNIVES, GUNS, POISONS, BUT YOU CAN'T MANAGE AN EVENING GOWN...?

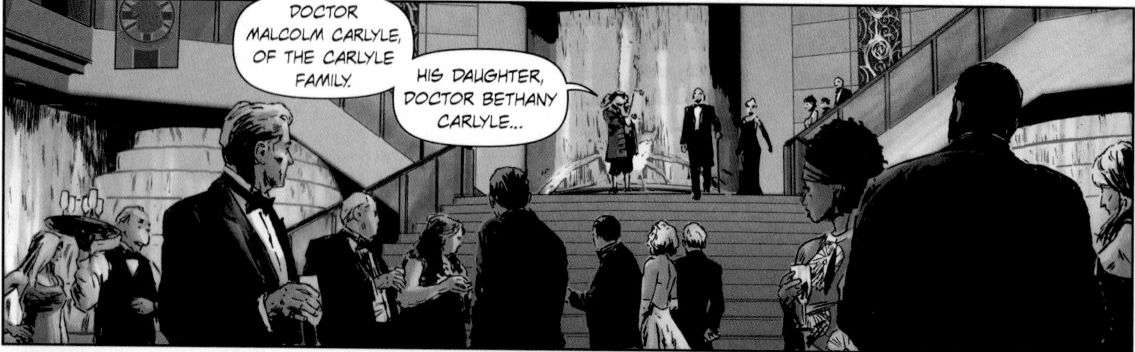
DOCTOR MALCOLM CARLYLE, OF THE CARLYLE FAMILY.
HIS DAUGHTER, DOCTOR BETHANY CARLYLE...

...HIS DAUGHTER, COMMANDER FOREVER CARLYLE.

DOCTOR JAMES MANN, TO THE CARLYLE FAMILY. SECRETARY ARTHUR COHN, TO THE CARLYLE FAMILY.

YOUR ROYAL HIGHNESSES.
MY FATHER WOULD BURST A VEIN, HE HEARD YOU SPEAKING TO US LIKE THAT, MALCOLM.
CHARLOTTE, YOU LOOK **EXQUISITE.**
THANKS TO **YOUR** PEOPLE, MALCOLM...
YOUR ROYAL HIGHNESS.
BETHANY, HOW NICE TO SEE YOU.
EDWARD, YOU REMEMBER JAMES MANN AND ARTHUR COHN.

MALCOLM! I'M DISAPPOINTED ABIGAIL DIDN'T JOIN YOU...
AS IS SHE, CHARLOTTE...
...HER HEALTH... CONCERNED...
COMMANDER...
...WONDERFUL TO SEE YOU **AGAIN.**
SIR THOMAS, A PLEASURE.

CAN I EXPECT YOU AT THE GAME TONIGHT?
IF MY FATHER WILL PERMIT IT.
OF COURSE.
YOU MET THE NEWEST ADDITION TO OUR EXCLUSIVE CLUB?
RAUSLING'S NEW LAZARUS? I HAVEN'T HAD THE PLEASURE.
CRISTOF MUELLER, CAPTAIN CRISTOF MUELLER, AS HE'LL BE THE FIRST TO REMIND YOU...
...STILL FULL OF PISS AND VINEGAR AND POSTURING. ONE OF US IS GOING TO HAVE TO EXPLAIN TO HIM HOW THINGS WORK.
YOU'RE THE MAN TO DO IT--
SIR THOMAS, I BEG YOUR PARDON...
...BUT I WAS WONDERING IF MISS CARLYLE MIGHT HONOR ME WITH A DANCE?
MY PARDON IS YOURS, JOACQUIM, BUT IT'S THE LADY'S DECISION, NOT MINE.
THERE'S NOBODY ON THE DANCE FLOOR.
THEN WE MUST BE BOLD AND LEAD THE WAY.

CHEERS, MATE.

EVERYONE IS STARING.
GOOD...
...THEY DAMN WELL SHOULD.

I DON'T KNOW HOW TO DANCE, JOACQUIM.

FOREVER.
OF COURSE YOU DO.

MALCOLM...
...MIGHT YOU HAVE A MOMENT TO SPEAK PRIVATELY LATER?
ABOUT BITTNER'S RELATIONSHIP TO CARLYLE, PERHAPS?
NOW IS AS GOOD A TIME AS ANY, SEVARA.
NOW MIGHT NOT BE THE BEST CHOICE...
...YOU MIGHT WANT TO WATCH WHAT JAKOB DOES NEXT.
I KNOW EXACTLY WHAT HE'S GOING TO DO NEXT, SEVARA.

THEY'LL BE IN SESSION ALL DAY TOMORROW, NO LAZARI ALLOWED.
WE COULD MEET AT THE GYM, OR THE POOL.
PERHAPS VISIT THE GALLERY?
I'D LIKE THAT VERY MUCH.
I SHOULD BE FREE BY **NOON...**
...I BEG YOUR PARDON?
SHE'S CUTTING **IN...**
...AT MY **REQUEST,** I FEAR.
I WAS HOPING COMMANDER CARLYLE WOULD **INDULGE** AN OLD MAN.
WOULD YOU **HONOR** ME WITH A **DANCE,** FOREVER?
I CAN HARDLY **REFUSE.**
I DON'T WISH TO BE **RUDE,** BUT ARE YOU SURE YOU WANT TO STAY ON YOUR **FEET?**
AH, YOU'RE REFERRING TO **THIS,** ARE YOU?

YOUR CONCERN FOR AN OLD MAN IS APPRECIATED, MY DEAR...
...BUT IT'S UNNECESSARY...
...AS YOU CAN SEE...
...I'M FEELING BETTER THAN I HAVE IN YEARS.
SHALL WE DANCE, MISS CARLYLE?

CARLYLE
ODERINT DUM METUANT

OWEN FREEMAN

CONCLAVE

CHAPTER THREE

57°03’57N, 0°54’51E – The North Sea
Facility: Triton One
Family: Armitage
Population [Family]: 0 [3 temporary]
FOREVER!
Population [Waste]: 420
Population [Serf]: 80
FOREVER, WAIT!
I HAVE TO FIND MY FATHER, JOACQUIM.
I HAVE TO TELL HIM WHAT'S HAPPENED.
I KNOW YOU DO.
I'LL WAIT FOR YOU AT SIR THOMAS' GAME.
PLEASE COME IF YOU CAN.

...YOUR TALK WITH SEVARA BITTNER GO?
THERE ARE SOME MINOR ISSUES OUTSTANDING...
...MOSTLY REGARDING TRADE AND PROPRIETARY TECH.
BUT SHE WILL COME OVER TO US?
PENDING THE OUTCOME OF THE CONCLAVE, YES.
JAMES AND BETHANY ARE ON THEIR WAY?
HERE, FATHER.
THIS COULDN'T WAIT UNTIL TOMORROW?
NO.
I NEED A CONFIRMATION BEFORE DELIBERATIONS BEGIN IN THE MORNING.
PROVIDED WE CAN DRAW A CLEAR SAMPLE THAT SHOULDN'T BE A PROBLEM.
THANK YOU, JAMES.
ARTHUR?
HOCK'S GOING TO KNOW THE GLASS WAS TAKEN, MALCOLM.
HE WON'T BE SURE, HE'LL THINK ONE OF THE WAITSTAFF CLEARED IT.
EVEN IF HE DOES, WHAT ARE HIS OPTIONS?
IF HE'S TRULY CAUGHT UP WITH US ON THE GENETICS, THIS WILL SIMPLY CONFIRM IT.
IF IT'S PHARMACEUTICAL MIMICRY, HE'LL SAY WE'RE TRYING TO DISCREDIT HIM.
I'VE BEEN WAITING YEARS FOR THIS, ARTHUR.
BELIEVE ME, I'VE ACCOUNTED FOR EVERYTHING.
FATHER!

THERE YOU ARE, I DIDN'T...YOU **LEFT** THE BALL, **EVERYONE** LEFT...
...SOMETHING **HAPPENED.** HOCK ASKED ME TO **DANCE** WITH HIM.
IN FRONT OF EVERYONE, **ALL** OF THE FAMILIES.
HE REMOVED THE **BRACES** ON HIS **LEGS,** HE DIDN'T **NEED** THEM.
I COULDN'T **REFUSE.**
OUR ALLIES, OUR ENEMIES... **ALL** OF THEM SAW IT...
...THEY ALL BELIEVE HE HAS WHAT WE HAVE, THAT HE TOOK IT FROM **JONAH--**
YEAH, NO KIDDING.
YOU KNEW IT WOULD HAPPEN.
YOU LET HIM HUMILIATE ME.
THAT WAS **NOT** THE INTENT.
OH, FOR THE LOVE OF GOD, FOREVER...
...SO OLD MAN HOCK PUT HIS PAWS ON YOU AND STARED AT YOUR **TITS** FROM POINT-BLANK RANGE.
BIG FUCKING DEAL.

YOU HUMILIATED YOURSELF WHEN YOU WENT TRAIPSING AROUND WITH JOACQUIM MORRAY.
JESUS CHRIST, YOU WERE PRACTICALLY RIDING HIM ON THE DANCE FLOOR.
I-- I WASN'T, I DIDN'T.
BETHANY ELIZABETH CARLYLE, THAT IS ENOUGH.
YOU WILL APOLOGIZE TO YOUR SISTER.
YOU WILL APOLOGIZE TO YOUR SISTER RIGHT THIS INSTANT.
IT'S THE TRUTH! WE ALL SAW IT!
NOW, BETHANY!
SORRY.

DON'T LISTEN TO HER.
SHE'S ANGRY BECAUSE SHE HAS TO WORK TONIGHT.
WE KNEW HOCK WOULD HAVE TO MAKE THE GAMBIT IN PUBLIC, FOREVER.
I THOUGHT YOU UNDERSTOOD THAT WOULD MEAN HE WOULD MAKE IT AS GRAND A GESTURE AS POSSIBLE.
IT'S MY FAULT, I SHOULD HAVE WARNED YOU.
I AM VERY SORRY.
IT'S... IT'S ALL RIGHT, FATHER.
THE NIGHT IS STILL YOUNG AND WE'VE WORK TO DO HERE.
YOU SHOULD GO OUT, ENJOY THE EVENING. I BELIEVE THERE'S A POKER GAME, SOMETHING LIKE THAT?
AT SIR THOMAS'S.
DON'T STAY OUT TOO LATE.

CHECK.
CHECK.
CHECK.
RAISE...

...TWO HUNDRED. WHO WILL STAY?
YOU'RE NOT LOSING ME THAT EASILY, MISTER LI. CALL.
YOU, JIAOLONG, ARE WHAT WE CALL A CHIP BULLY.

WE HAVE NOT EVEN REACHED THE DRAW YET!
TRUE, CAPTAIN MUELLER...
...AND IF YOU WISH TO SEE IT, YOU WILL PAY FOR THE PRIVILEGE.
WE'RE IN--

--I MEAN SONJA'S IN. THAT'S WHAT I MEAN.
SAY, "CALL."
YES, I AM IN.
CALL!
I WILL CALL ALSO.
YOUR LUCK CANNOT CONTINUE.
I DON'T THINK IT'S LUCK, CRISTOFF.
I'LL CALL.
RIGHT, THEN, LET'S HEAR IT, MY FINE AND FANCY LAZARI...
...WHO WANTS HOW MANY?
COME, JOIN US IN THE PEANUT GALLERY.
YOU KNOW BIR CHIKKU MEHTA, OF COURSE.
I DO, WE MET WHEN MINETTA VISITED IN '61. YOU'RE WELL, BIR?
I AM DRUNK ON SIR THOMAS' WHISKEY, SO I AM VERY WELL, INDEED.
AND YOU MUST BE ALIMAH.
ASSALAMU ALAIKUM.
WA ALAIKUM ASSALAM.

IT IS A GREAT HONOR TO MEET YOU, COMMANDER CARLYLE.
PLEASE, JUST FOREVER. I'M NOT SURE HONOR IS THE WO--
BUT IT IS! I STUDIED EVERY LAZARUS FOR MY TRAINING, ALL OF THEM.
YOU ARE AMAZING!
NO, I'M BLUSHING.
I STILL PRACTICE ON THE VASSALOVKA INFIL-EXFIL SIMULATION YOUR FATHER GAVE--
SCHWANZLUTSCHER!
SIX TIMES NOW! SIX TIMES IN A ROW THE LITTLE CRIPPLE DOES THIS!
A FULL HOUSE! FOUR OF A KIND! A STRAIGHT, THEN ANOTHER FULL HOUSE!
YOU RELY TOO MUCH ON YOUR BLUFF, CAPTAIN.
YOU THINK I AM BLUFFING? FICK DICH, YOU PLATE OF SHIT!
EASY, MEU CAPITÃO, WE'RE ALL FRIENDS HERE.
WE ARE NOT!

YOU ARE D'SOUZA'S LAZARUS, ZEFERINO!
YOU AND SONJA AND I, WE ARE ALLIES, YET WE SIT HERE, DRINKING ARMITAGE'S LIQUOR, EATING ARMITAGE'S FOOD--
--AND ALL AROUND US ARE OUR ENEMIES--
SHOULD WE...?
NO.
--AND WE PRETEND WE ARE FRIENDS, AND WHY? SO THIS GENETIC MISTAKE CAN ROB US?
I COULD BREAK YOU WITH ONE HAND. IT WOULD BE A FAVOR TO YOUR FAMILY.
MISTER MUELLER, YOU WILL NOT--
THOMAS, PLEASE.
I DO NOT CHEAT. I DO NOT NEED TO.
YOU DREW FOR THE STRAIGHT AND ENDED UP WITH GARBAGE.
THIS IS THE THIRD TIME YOU'VE TRIED THAT AND FAILED. YOU'RE A SLOW LEARNER.
AS FAR AS THAT GOES...
...WENING COULD HAVE TAKEN THIS HAND, BUT SHE CUT HERSELF OUT OF A FULL HOUSE WHEN SHE DISCARDED HER SEVEN.
OH MOTHERFUCK!

NOW LET'S TALK ABOUT YOU. MUELLER, CRISTOFF, THIRTY-ONE, WASTE-BORN, PARENTS DECEASED, FATHER UNKNOWN...
...SELECTED FOR RAUSLING MILITARY SERVICE. BROUGHT TO THE FAMILY'S ATTENTION FOR MERIT WHILE SERVING WITH MARTINS AGAINST NKOSI...
...SELECTED LAZARUS AFTER SIX-MONTH TRIAL FOLLOWING THE DEATH OF YOUR PREDECESSOR, CASPAR WOLF.
I COMPLETED A SPECTROGRAPHIC ANALYSIS OF YOUR PERSPIRATION AND RESPIRATION OVER AN HOUR AGO.
YOU'RE SWIMMING IN A SOUP. THREE TOCOPHEROLS, TWO TOCOTRIENOLS, TWO SARMS, ALL COURTESY OF DOCTOR HOCK'S BENEVOLENCE...
...IT'S A LOT OF ENHANCEMENT, AT LEAST FOR ONE KIND OF PERFORMANCE.
IT ALSO ACCOUNTS FOR YOUR DIFFICULTY CONTROLLING YOUR TEMPER.
I'VE ALSO MATCHED THE TRACES OF PERFUME ON YOUR SKIN AND CLOTHING...
...THAT, COMBINED WITH ONE OR TWO OF THE OTHER DRUGS IN YOUR SYSTEM IS... SHALL WE SAY, SUGGESTIVE.
SHALL I NAME THE LADY IN QUESTION? OR WOULD YOU RATHER APOLOGIZE FOR CALLING ME A PLATE OF SHIT?
I APOLOGIZE FOR MY ACCUSATIONS AND BEHAVIOR, MISTER LI.

YOU HAVE NO IDEA HOW LUCKY YOU JUST GOT.
YOU HAVE NO IDEA WHAT JIAOLONG CAN DO.
YOU'RE WRONG ABOUT SOMETHING ELSE, MATE.
WE MAY NOT ALL OF US BE FRIENDS, BUT WE'RE THE CLOSEST WE'VE GOT.
WE'RE LAZARI, AND THAT MAKES US DIFFERENT FROM EVERYONE ELSE IN WAYS THEY WILL NEVER UNDERSTAND.
WE KNOW OUR LOYALTIES, SAME AS WE KNOW THE PURPOSE WE SERVE TO OUR RESPECTIVE FAMILIES.
WE MAY ALL BE SET TO KILLING EACH OTHER BEFORE THIS IS OVER.
WE'LL ALL DO AS WE'RE ORDERED.
DOESN'T MEAN WE'LL HAVE TO LIKE IT.

SONJA, I BELIEVE IT'S **YOUR** DEAL....
I'M THINKING OF TAKING A WALK.
WOULD YOU CARE TO JOIN ME?

...THREE, THREE, THREE...
...FOUR, FOUR, FOUR, FOUR...

...FOUR, FOUR, FIVE, FIVE, FIVE...

THE WEATHER'S TURNING.
IT LOOKS LIKE A STORM.
IS THAT WHY YOU'RE NERVOUS?
THERE'S TALK THAT YOUR FAMILY WILL GO BACK TO HOCK.
IT WILL NOT HAPPEN.
I WOULD VERY MUCH LIKE TO KISS YOU.
WOULD YOU PERMIT ME TO KISS YOU, FOREVER?
PLEASE.

I HOPE... I HOPE THAT WAS ALL RIGHT.
YES.
I WAS AFRAID... I WAS AFRAID I WOULD TASTE OF METAL AND OIL.
THAT IS NOT HOW YOU TASTE.

DID I DO IT RIGHT?
OH, YES.
VERY WELL, INDEED.
YOU'RE MY FIRST KISS.
AND SECOND.
MAY I BE YOUR THIRD?
JOACQUIM.
I MAY NOT WANT TO STOP.
I MAY NOT WANT YOU TO.

THERE YOU ARE!
HELLO, SONJA.
I LOOKED FOR YOU IN THE GYM BUT YOU WERE NOT THERE.
MAY I... AM I INTERRUPTING? YOU WISHED TO BE ALONE?
NOT AT ALL. PLEASE, SIT.
I JUST SAW XOLANI, HE SAYS THEY ARE STILL IN CONFERENCE.
FIVE HOURS NOW, NO ONE HAS COME IN OR OUT OF THE ROOM.
IT'S ONLY THE FIRST DAY.
I'M SURE IT TOOK FIVE HOURS JUST TO GET THROUGH EVERYONE'S OPENING STATEMENTS...
...MIGHT WE GET A FRESH POT OF TEA, AND A CUP FOR MY FRIEND, PLEASE?
CERTAINLY, COMMANDER.
HOW WAS THE REST OF YOUR EVENING?
XOLANI SAID THAT JIAOLONG TOOK US ALL UP BY THE ANKLES AND SHOOK UNTIL EVEN THE LOOSE CHANGE FELL FROM OUR POCKETS.
BUT I WON A HAND!

I DID NOT SEE YOU LEAVE. YOU AND JOACQUIM.
MAY I ASK...YOU AND HE ARE...?
I THINK SO? I HOPE SO?
I VERY MUCH HOPE YOUR BROTHER WILL BE RETURNED SAFELY, THEN.
THANK YOU.
THAT THERE WILL BE NO ESCALATION, NO NEED FOR A TRIAL.
WHAT DO YOU MEAN?
IT IS NOTHING, I AM SPEAKING RUMORS, FORGIVE ME.
WHAT RUMORS? WHAT HAVE YOU HEARD?
MY SISTER AND TIAGO D'SOUZA SHARED BREAKFAST THIS MORNING.
I HEARD THEM SAYING, IF DOCTOR HOCK HAS WHAT YOUR FAMILY HAS, MORRAY WILL RETURN TO...TO OUR ALLIANCE.
IT IS ONLY WHAT I HEARD, MY SISTER AND REMIGIO D'SOUZA'S YOUNGEST, THEY ARE NOT PRIVY TO--
TING-TING-TIN
BA-DEET BA-DEET
THEY'VE ADJOURNED.

...THERE'S DEFINITELY SOME OF OUR WORK IN HIS SYSTEM, NO QUESTION...
...BUT IT'S GOING TO BE VERY DIFFICULT TO PROVE WHAT'S PROPRIETARY AND WHAT ISN'T.
WITHOUT A SMOKING DNA STRAND IT WON'T STICK, MALCOLM.
HOCK'LL RESPOND BY REMINDING EVERYONE THAT HE WAS PART OF THE LONGEVITY PROJECT BACK IN THE BEGINNING, THAT HE CODED SOME OF THE ORIGINAL SEQUENCES WORKING WITH ABBY.
HE'LL CLAIM THIS IS THE BY-PRODUCT OF THAT WORK...
...THAT IT'S NOT STOLEN BUT EARNED.
NOT IDEAL, BUT EXPECTED.
FOREVER, COME WITH ME, PLEASE.
YES, FATHER.

CLOSE THE DOOR.
SIT WITH ME.
FATHER? IS EVERYTHING ALL RIGHT?
I NEED YOU TO DO SOMETHING, SOMETHING ONLY YOU CAN DO.
IT'S GOING TO BE DIFFICULT. IT'S GOING TO BE DANGEROUS.
AND YOU MUST DO IT FLAWLESSLY, DAUGHTER.
I CANNOT EMPHASIZE THAT ENOUGH, FOREVER. THERE IS NO ROOM FOR ERROR OR HESITATION.
BELIEVE ME WHEN I SAY EITHER WILL BRING RUIN TO OUR FAMILY.
TELL ME AND I SHALL DO IT.
THAT'S MY GIRL.
ONCE ALL THE FAMILIES ARE BACK IN SESSION TOMORROW...

"...THAT'S WHEN
YOU'LL DO IT..."

...fuckers...
...you fuckers...
...I just... I don't want to be hurt anymore...
IT'S FUNNY.
I'VE THOUGHT THE SAME THING MORE TIMES THAN I CAN COUNT.
FOREVER!
OH GOD, OH THANK GOD...
...I'M SORRY, I'M SORRY FOR EVERYTHING...
...I'M SO SORRY--
SO AM I, JONAH.
SO AM I.
CHKSSS

CARLYLE
ODERINT DUM METUANT

OWEN FREEMAN

CONCLAVE

CHAPTER FOUR

57°03’57N, 0°54’51E – The North Sea
Facility: Triton One

TUNK
TUNK
TUNG

SECTION 06

whrr?
Forever?

WH-WHAT--
OW OW--

--OW
FOREVER
STOP--

--WHAT ARE
YOU DOING
STOP--

--STOP
OH GOD OH
MY GOD...
...OH MY
GOD...

...HE DIDN'T SEND YOU TO **RESCUE** ME...
...HE SENT YOU TO **KILL** ME.

FATHER SENT YOU TO KILL ME.

YES.

I DON'T WANT TO DIE.
PLEASE, FOREVER, I DON'T WANT TO DIE, I D--

--AH!
FUCK YOU!

WHAT YOU WANT?
YOU THINK I CARE WHAT YOU FUCKING WANT?
I SHOULD'VE KILLED YOU ALREADY, YOU'RE ALIVE BECAUSE OF WHAT I WANT!
ANY SECOND NOW HOCK'S DRUG-MONKEY IS GOING TO DISCOVER YOU'RE GONE--
--AND THE MOMENT HE HITS THE ALARM, THAT'S IT, IT'S OVER FOR YOU.
FOREVER, PLEASE--
I PUT A BULLET IN YOU AND DUMP YOU TO THE OCEAN FLOOR.
YOU'RE ALIVE RIGHT NOW ONLY BECAUSE I WANT ANSWERS, JONAH.
YOU BETRAYED YOUR FAMILY--
I KNOW, PLEASE--
--PLOTTED TO MURDER OUR FATHER, TO MURDER ME--
--I'M SORRY, I'M SO SORRY FOREVER--
--BEAT JOHANNA HALF TO DEATH--
--I'M SO--
--WH-WHAT? WAIT--

--TO START A WAR--
--WITH MORRAY, YOUR FUCKING COUP--
--FOREVER, I DIDN'T, I SWEAR TO GOD--
--I NEVER HIT HER!
I SWEAR TO GOD, I SWEAR TO GOD, FOREVER, I WOULD NEVER HURT JO.
SHE TOOK CARE OF ME, SHE'S THE ONLY ONE WHO EVER DID.
ON 07
I DID IT, I DID EVERYTHING YOU SAY, I DID IT ALL.
I DID IT FOR HER.

SECTION 07
DID JO SEND ME THIS?
TO: CARLYLE_FOREVER
FROM: %#%UNKNOWN#(&%ERROR
HE IS NOT YOUR FATHER.
THIS IS NOT YOUR FAMILY.
I DON'T KNOW.
MAYBE. SHE COULD HAVE.
IS IT *TRUE?*
SECTION 07
IS IT TRUE?
IT'S **NOT** AS SIMPLE AS THAT.
BULLSHIT!

IT EITHER IS OR IT ISN'T!
I'M EITHER MY FATHER'S DAUGHTER OR I'M NOT!
FOREVER, YOU WERE GROWN IN A FUCKING LAB!
BETHANY AND JAMES MADE YOU TO FATHER'S ORDER!
YOU'RE NOT HIS DAUGHTER.
YOU'RE HIS TOOL.
I... I SHOULDN'T HAVE SAID THAT.
HE LOVES YOU, I KNOW HE DOES.
MORE THAN HE DOES US.

THANK YOU FOR TELLING ME THE TRUTH, JONAH.

IT'S MY TURN TO SAY THAT I'M SORRY.
I HAVE TO DO THIS.
FOREVER...

YOU DON'T.
YOU DON'T HAVE TO DO WHAT HE TELLS YOU.

I DO.
IT... HURTS WHEN I DON'T, JONAH.

IT'S THE DRUGS, THE MEDICINE THEY GIVE YOU. OXYTOCIN, OTHER THINGS, I DON'T EVEN KNOW WHAT THEY ARE.
TO MAKE YOU LOVE US. TO MAKE YOU LOYAL TO US.

I WANT TO LIVE, FOREVER.
I KNOW I'M SHIT, I KNOW WHAT I'VE DONE CAN'T BE FORGIVEN.
BUT I'VE SEEN THINGS, I UNDERSTAND THINGS I DIDN'T BEFORE...
...I NEVER LOVED YOU THE WAY YOU LOVED US, WE BOTH KNOW THAT.
BUT IF YOU LET ME LIVE, I WILL NEVER GIVE YOU CAUSE TO REGRET IT. I WILL BE YOUR BROTHER.
PLEASE, I'M BEGGING YOU--
DEEETDEEETDEEET DEEETDEEETDEEETDEEE
SECTION 07

IT'S TOO LATE, THEY KNOW YOU'RE GONE.
I HAVE TO MAKE IT LOOK LIKE HOCK DID IT, DO YOU UNDERSTAND?
IT'S WHAT FATHER TOLD ME TO DO.
AND WE MUST ALWAYS DO AS WE'RE TOLD.

SECTION 07

IN CASE OF EMERGENCY
FOR COLD WEATHER EVACUATION
SURVIVAL IMMERSION SUIT

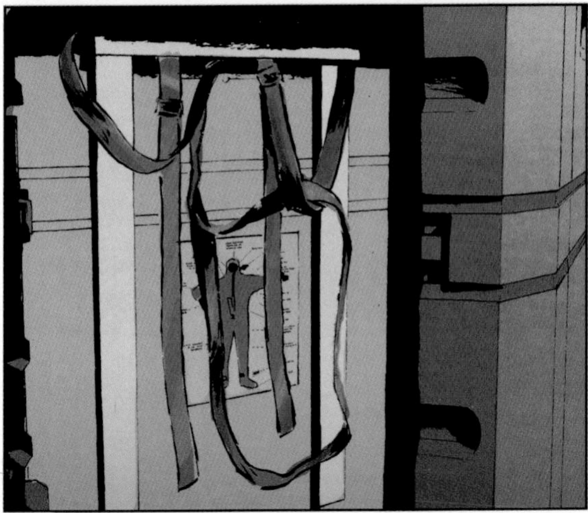

--YOU CAN INFLATE IT, LIKE A ONE-MAN LIFE RAFT!
WHAT?
THERE'S A TAB, YOU PULL IT AND THE SUIT WILL INFLATE!
YOU'LL BE ABLE TO FLOAT!
OKAY!
YOU NEED TO STAY UNDER FOR AS LONG AS YOU CAN! THERE'S AIR IN THE SUIT, YOU'LL BE FINE!
YOU'LL SINK WHEN YOU HIT THE WATER! DON'T FIGHT IT! THE SUIT CAN TAKE IT!
I UNDERSTAND!
I REMOVED THE BEACON AND THE LIGHT! THE STORM WILL CONCEAL YOU!
EVEN IF YOU CATCH THE CURRENT IT'S A LONG TIME IN THE WATER BEFORE YOU REACH LAND! CONSERVE YOUR STRENGTH!
ARE YOU GOING TO BE ALL RIGHT?

THE WHOLE FACILITY IS GOING INTO LOCKDOWN! STANDARD SECURITY PRECAUTION, THEY'LL HAVE CONFINED ALL FAMILIES AND STAFF TO THEIR QUARTERS WHILE THEY CONDUCT THE SEARCH!
I'LL BE FINE!
YOU COULD DROWN, JONAH!
THIS MAY NOT EVEN WORK!
IS IT SCARY, FOREVER?
WHEN YOU DIE?
ONLY THE FIRST TIME.
THANK YOU, FOREVER.

FOREVER!
WE WERE STARTING TO WORRY.
ARMITAGE'S PEOPLE HAVE COMPLETED THEIR PRELIMINARY INVESTIGATION.
THEY'RE LIFTING THE LOCKDOWN, EVERYONE -- FAMILIES AND THEIR STAFF AND LAZARI -- ARE BEING SUMMONED TO THE GREAT HALL.
YOU NEED TO GET CHANGED.
I'VE LAID OUT YOUR PILLS FOR YOU.
FOREVER?
ARE YOU ALL RIGHT? HOW ARE YOU FEELING?
FINE, JAMES.
I FEEL FINE.

WHERE IS EVERYONE?
THEY'VE GONE AHEAD.
I WANTED TO WAIT FOR YOU.
ARMITAGE RELEASED A PRELIMINARY REPORT.
THEY FOUND JONAH'S BLOOD IN THE HOCK SUITE. SIGNS OF TAMPERING WITH THE ACCESS PANELS.
HOCK'S MAN BEAT HIM.
I'M NOT SURPRISED.
I ASSUME IT WAS YOU WHO STOLE THE EVACUATION SUIT?
YES, SIR.
THAT WAS INSPIRED.
NOW IT LOOKS LIKE HOCK WAS TRYING TO COVER HIS TRACKS, AN ATTEMPT TO MAKE IT APPEAR THAT JONAH ESCAPED.
I KNOW THIS WAS DIFFICULT, EVE. I KNOW IT HURT. HE WAS YOUR BROTHER.
HE WAS MY SON.
BUT WE'RE ALMOST THROUGH, JUST ONE THING REMAINS...

"...AND I KNOW YOU WON'T LET ME DOWN...."
I WANT TO BEGIN BY FIRST APOLOGIZING FOR THE INCONVENIENCE OF THE LOCK DOWN AND TO THANK EVERYONE FOR THEIR PATIENCE WHILE SECURITY INVESTIGATED THIS MATTER.
AS YOU ARE ALL AWARE, JONAH CARLYLE HAS DISAPPEARED. SECURITY HAS NOW COMPLETED THEIR REVIEW OF SURVEILLANCE FOOTAGE AND THEIR SEARCH OF THE STATION.
AS ARBITER AND HOST TO THIS CONCLAVE, I AM NOW PREPARED TO RELAY THEIR FINDINGS:
FIRST, THAT A SEARCH OF THE HOCK SUITE REVEALED BLOOD TRACES MATCHING MISTER CARLYLE.
SECOND, THAT THE MAINTENANCE ACCESS IN THE HOCK SUITE SHOWED SIGNS OF TAMPERING BOTH WITHIN AND TO THE EXTERIOR OF THIS FACILITY.
THIRD, THAT DURING THE SEARCH ONE OF THE EMERGENCY IMMERSION SUITS USED FOR EVACUATION WAS FOUND TO BE MISSING.
AND FOURTH, THAT NO SIGN OF MISTER CARLYLE APPEARS ON ANY SURVEILLANCE FOOTAGE.
THIS LAST BEING QUALIFIED BY THE FACT THAT FAMILY SUITES ARE NOT SUBJECT TO SURVEILLANCE, BUT ONLY THE COMMON AREAS.
IN VIEW OF THESE FINDINGS, IT IS MY CONCLUSION THAT MISTER CARLYLE IS NO LONGER ABOARD TRITON ONE.
FURTHER, GIVEN THE PURPOSE OF THIS CONCLAVE TO NEGOTIATE HIS SAFE RETURN TO HIS FAMILY, THIS GATHERING MUST NOW TURN ITS ATTENTION TO THE MATTER OF HIS DISAPPEARANCE.
DOCTOR HOCK, MISTER CARLYLE WAS IN YOUR CARE, AND HIS SAFETY YOUR RESPONSIBILITY.
WHAT DO YOU OFFER IN YOUR DEFENSE?
I NEED NO DEFENSE, YOUR HIGHNESS!
THIS IS A GAMBIT BY CARLYLE TO DISCREDIT ME, TO SCUTTLE THESE TALKS, NOTHING LESS!

HE'S SCARED.
FOR SIXTY YEARS HE'S COWED YOU WITH A PROMISE OF LONGEVITY, AND NOW I HAVE WHAT HE HELD. HE KNOWS HIS POWER OVER YOU IS LOST.
I CAN GIVE YOU EVERYTHING CARLYLE HAS PROMISED AND THEN WITHHELD.
I CAN FREE YOU FROM HIS SCIENTIFIC TYRANNY...
...IF YOU STAND WITH ME AND MY ALLIES, INSTEAD OF WITH A MAN WHO WILL MURDER HIS OWN SON IN AN ATTEMPT TO DISCREDIT ME.
YOU SON OF A BITCH--
FATHER!
MALCOLM!
THAT'S WHAT THIS IS ABOUT, JAKOB?
TECHNOLOGY YOU STOLE FROM MY SON'S BODY?
AND THAT'S WHY HE HAD HIM MURDERED, AND THAT'S WHY HE HAD HIM DUMPED IN THE SEA.
TO HIDE THE PROOF.

MALCOLM, INDUSTRIAL ESPIONAGE IS ONE OF OUR GRAVEST CRIMES AS DEFINED BY THE ACCORDS.
THE THEFT OF A FAMILY'S SOURCE OF WEALTH, IF SUBSTANTIATED, IS GROUNDS FOR WAR.
THE PROOF IS VIBRATING THROUGH HIS CELLS.
GIVE ME A BLOOD SAMPLE AND TWENTY-FOUR HOURS AND I'LL PROVE IT TO EVERYONE.
YOU WILL MANUFACTURE THE PROOF, YOU MEAN.
THERE WOULD BE NO LONGEVITY CODE WITHOUT ME, MALCOLM, OR HAVE YOU FORGOTTEN?
WITNESS HIS ARROGANCE! HE REFUSES TO ACKNOWLEDGE THAT MY WORK COULD HAVE REPLICATED HIS OWN.
ANY TEST WOULD BE INCONCLUSIVE...
...SO I WOULD OFFER ANOTHER MEANS OF RESOLVING THIS MATTER.
THE MACAU ACCORDS ALLOW IT.
YOUR CHAMPION AGAINST MY OWN.
YOU HAVE NO LAZARUS.
TRUE.
BUT I HAVE ALLIES.

WHO IS WILLING TO STAND AS MY CHAMPION?

YOU WERE A LITTLE SLOW IN COMING TO MY DEFENSE, MY DEAR...
...JUST LIKE YOUR MOTHER WAS A LITTLE SLOW IN SHIFTING ALLEGIANCE.

LET'S HOPE YOU'RE FASTER FIGHTING FOR YOUR LIFE.

CARLYLE
ODERINT DUM METUANT

CHAPTER FIVE

HERE FOLLOW THE CHARGES:
THAT HOCK DID ENGAGE IN INDUSTRIAL ESPIONAGE.
THAT HOCK DID STEAL TECHNOLOGY PROPRIETARY TO CARLYLE.
THAT HOCK THEN DID MURDER JONAH CARLYLE IN AN ATTEMPT TO CONCEAL THEIR CRIME.
TO DEFEND THEIR NAME, HOCK HAS DEMANDED TRIAL BY COMBAT.
HOCK WILL NAME THEIR CHAMPION.
MY FAMILY HAS NO LAZARUS TO CHAMPION OUR NAME.
OUR CLOSEST ALLY HAS EVER BEEN THE FAMILY BITTNER.
THEIR LAZARUS, SONJA BITTNER, WILL FIGHT FOR HOCK'S NAME...
...AND IN THE DEFEAT OF CARLYLE'S CHAMPION, WILL PROVE OUR INNOCENCE.
CARLYLE ANSWERS THIS CHALLENGE.
OUR DAUGHTER, FOREVER, STANDS IN OUR NAME.

THE COMBATANTS ARE NAMED AND THE PARTIES AGREED.
THE RESULT OF THIS COMBAT WILL BE BINDING.
THE CHAMPIONS WILL MAKE READY.
ALL OTHERS WILL WITHDRAW TO OBSERVE THE TRIAL FROM THE GALLERY...
...REFRESHMENTS WILL BE SERVED.
WE BEGIN IN FIVE MINUTES.

HE DID IT ON PURPOSE.
HOCK PICKED SONJA BECAUSE HE KNOWS YOU HAVE BECOME **FRIENDS...**

...JUST AS HE KNOWS THAT BITTNER PLANS TO ALLY WITH US AFTER THE CONCLAVE.
HE'S REMINDING SONJA THAT HOCK AND BITTNER FORCES ARE STILL FULLY **INTEGRATED...**

...SAYING THAT HE WILL **ORDER** HIS SOLDIERS TO **TURN** THEIR WEAPONS ON BITTNER IF SHE FAILS TO **KILL** YOU...

DETAILING PRECISELY WHAT HE WILL DO TO HER MOTHER AND SISTER IF SHE THROWS THE FIGHT.

SHE'S GOING TO TRY TO KILL YOU, FOREVER--
A POINT OF **ORDER...**

...THE TERMS OF THIS TRIAL MUST BE SET.
HOCK WILL SURRENDER ALL RESEARCH AND TECHNOLOGY RELATED TO THE CARLYLE LONGEVITY CODE.
THIS INCLUDES ANY BY-PRODUCT THAT YOU YOURSELF MAY CURRENTLY BENEFIT FROM.
THE TERMS ARE PLAIN, DOCTOR HOCK. SONJA BITTNER FIGHTS FOR YOUR INNOCENCE.
SHOULD SHE LOSE, YOUR GUILT IS DECIDED.
THAT IS UNDERSTOOD.
BUT WHAT IF WE WIN?
THEN YOU HAVE PROVEN YOUR INNOCENCE.
THAT IS NOT ENOUGH! IF HOCK IS INNOCENT, THEN CARLYLE IS GUILTY!
THEY WILL HAVE SLANDERED OUR NAME! THEY WILL HAVE VIOLATED THE PEACE OF THIS CONCLAVE!
IN VICTORY, WHAT WOULD HOCK DEMAND?
HER.

TO THE VICTOR, THE SPOILS.
YOUR DAUGHTER WILL BECOME OURS. IN DEATH, WE CLAIM HER BODY...
...IF ALIVE, WE CLAIM HER SERVICE.
THE DEMAND IS ABSURD, YOUR HIGHNESS.
ABSURD IT MAY BE, MALCOLM, BUT HE HAS A POINT.
BY THE TERMS OF THE TRIAL, EACH OF YOU FIGHTS FOR YOUR INNOCENCE. GUILT LAYS WITH THE DEFEATED.
THE TERMS ARE SET.
LET THE TRIAL BEGIN.

I HAVE NO CHOICE.

WE NEVER DO.

YOU'RE MY **FRIEND.**

NOT **TODAY.**

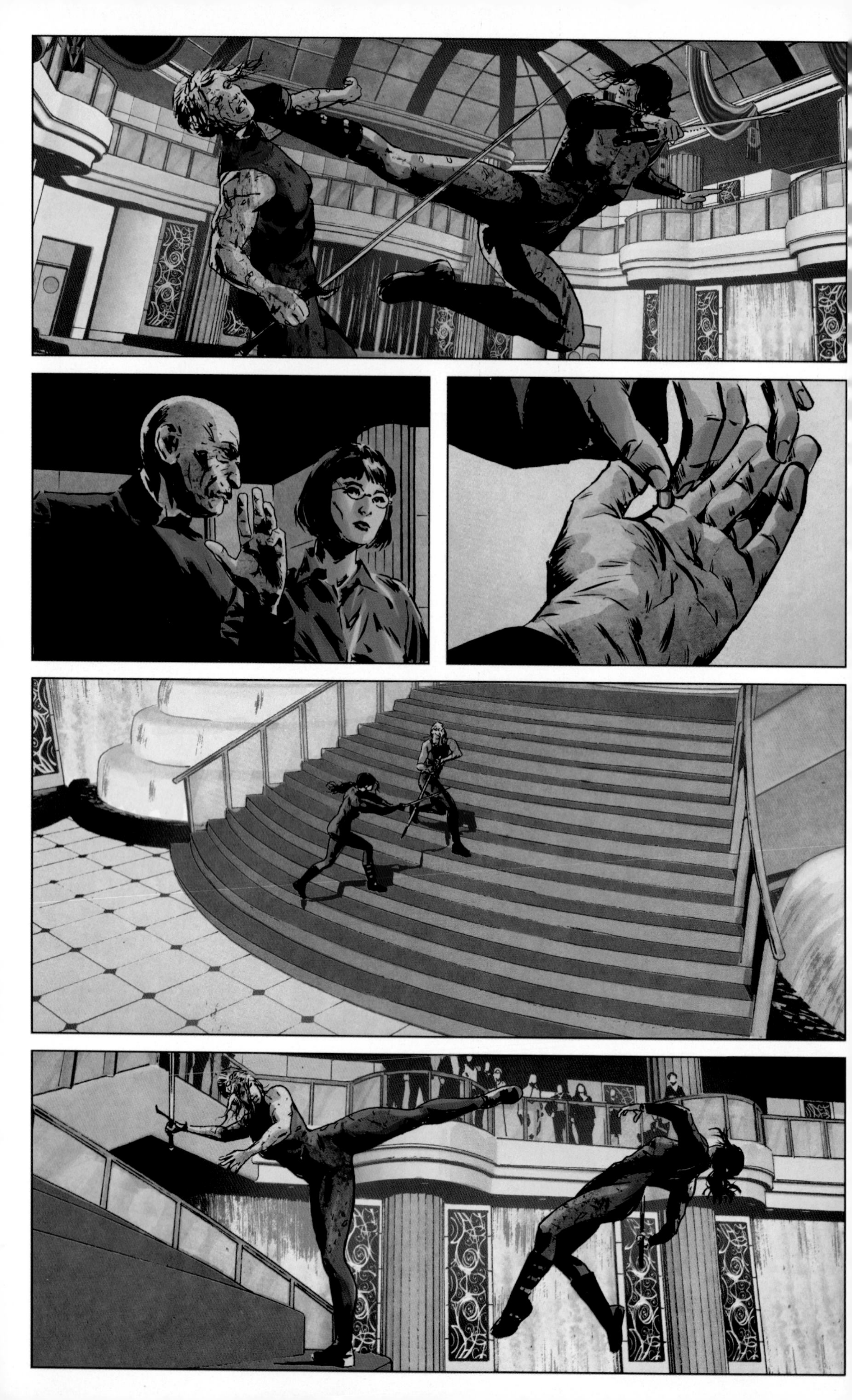

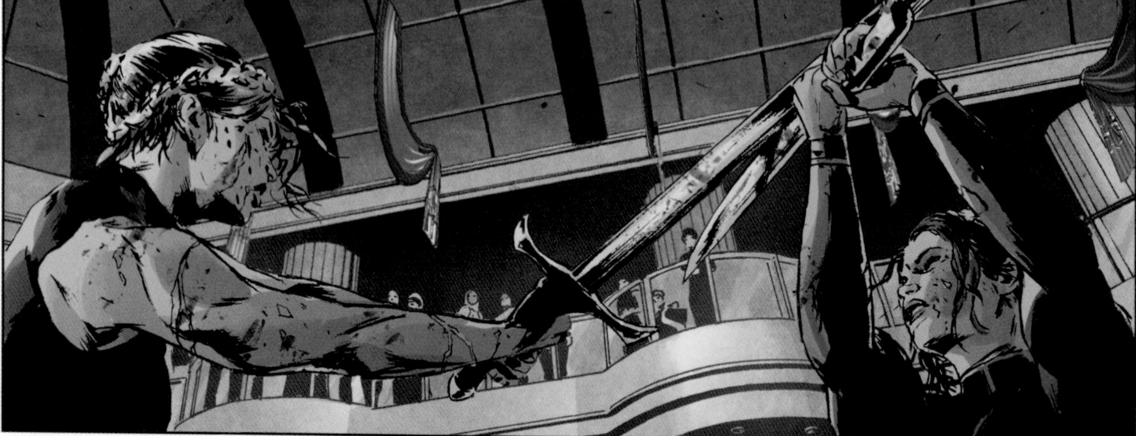

STOP!

IT'S OVER, EVERYONE CAN SEE THAT!

STAY YOUR DAUGHTER'S HAND AND SPARE MINE!

YOUR SWORD IS SO LIGHT.
I DID NOT KNOW WHAT I WAS DOING WITH IT.

YOU KNEW ENOUGH TO MAKE ME PAY TO GET IT BACK.
AH... DO... DO NOT MAKE ME LAUGH....

HOCK MUST YIELD.
TO YOU? NEVER.
YOUR CHAMPION IS DEFEATED. THE TRIAL IS CONCLUDED.
THAT YOU DO NOT WISH TO COST YOUR NEW ALLY HER LAZARUS IS OF NO CONCERN TO ME.
THIS TRIAL ENDS IN DEATH.
I APPEAL TO THE ARBITER OF THIS CONCLAVE. YOUR HIGHNESS, A JUDGEMENT, PLEASE.
NOWHERE IN THE TERMS OF THIS FIGHT NOR IN THE WORDS OF THE ACCORDS DOES TRIAL BY COMBAT REQUIRE THE DEATH OF A CHAMPION.
WE MUST THEREFORE AGREE WITH CARLYLE IN THIS, AND CALL THIS TRIAL ENDED.
FAMILY HOCK IS FOUND GUILTY OF THE CRIMES AS CHARGED.
THEY WILL SURRENDER ALL THAT WHICH THEY HAVE STOLEN...
...OR FACE THE CONSEQUENCES....

FUCK YOU.
THAT IS ALL I WILL GIVE YOU.
THAT AND NOTHING MORE.
I REFUSE THE RESULTS OF THIS TRIAL. I DEFY THIS CONCLAVE, THIS CHARADE.
IF THIS IS GROUNDS FOR WAR, SO BE IT.
I SPEAK FOR ALL WHO OPPOSE YOUR TYRANNY.
WE WOULD BURN THIS WORLD BEFORE WE SEE IT FALL TO CARLYLE.

MISTER COHN, TAKE JAMES AND MY SISTER AND CLEAR THE SUITE.
I'LL GET MY FATHER SAFELY TO THE PLANE.
FOREVER--
HOCK JUST DECLARED WAR, BETHANY.
MOVE. NOW--
Fo-rev-
-errrrr
FATHER!
JAMES! HELP HIM!
FATHER? PLEASE, FATHER...
...SAY SOMETHING...
...PLEASE, DADDY...
...PLEASE....

CARLYLE
ODERINT DUM METUANT

For more **LAZARUS** info, visit the digital letter column at http://familycarlyle.tumblr.com/

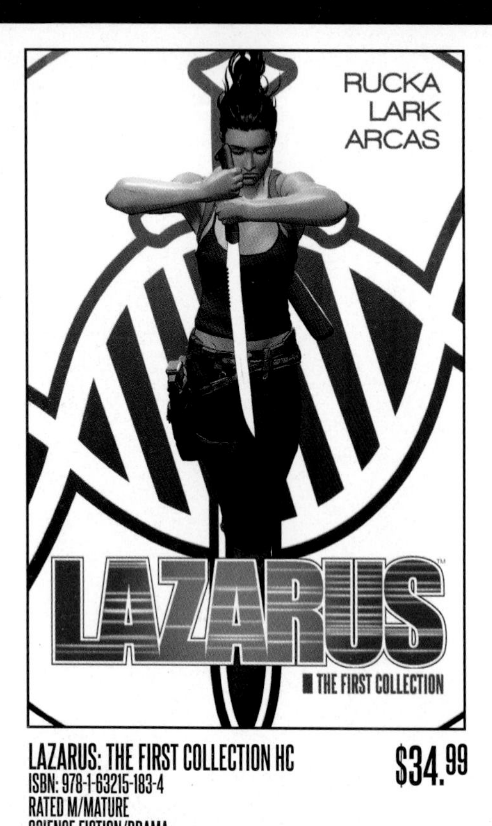

AVAILABLE FROM IMAGE COMICS.

Catch up on **LAZARUS**—the acclaimed science fiction series created by **GREG RUCKA** and **MICHAEL LARK**—in a handsome hardcover volume (featuring nearly 40 pages of bonus material). Available in fine comic and bookstores now.

LAZARUS: THE FIRST COLLECTION HC **$34.99**
ISBN: 978-1-63215-183-4
RATED M/MATURE
SCIENCE FICTION/DRAMA

ALSO AVAILABLE IN TRADE PAPERBACK EDITIONS....

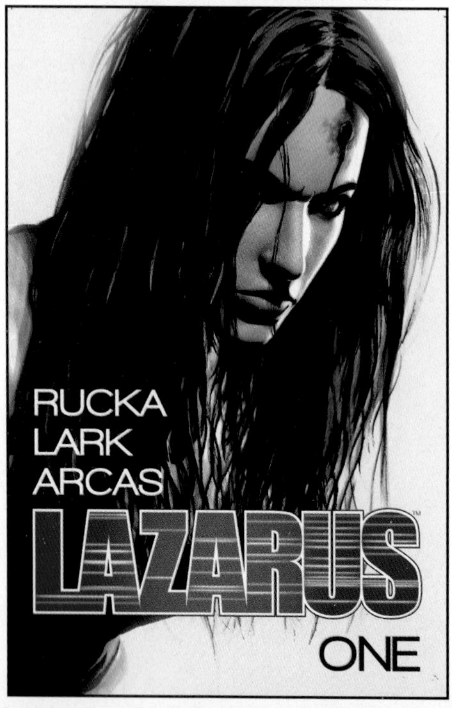

RUCKA
LARK
ARCAS
LAZARUS
TWO

LAZARUS VOL.1: FAMILY **$9.99**
ISBN: 978-1-60706-809-9
RATED M/MATURE
SCIENCE FICTION/DRAMA

LAZARUS VOL.2: LIFT **$14.99**
ISBN: 978-1-60706-871-6
RATED M/MATURE
SCIENCE FICTION/DRAMA